THIRSTY THURSDAY

Phyllis Root

illustrated by Helen Craig

WALKER BOOKS
AND SUBSIDIARIES
LONDON · BOSTON · SYDNEY · AUCKLAND

One Thursday on Bonnie Bumble's farm, everyone was thirsty. Especially the flowers.

The snapdragons
snapped.

The tiger lilies
growled.

The
Johnny jump-ups
jumped up
and down.

And the
black-eyed Susans
were spoiling
for a fight.

But the clouds refused
to even drop by.

At last
a little cloud
blew past.

Luckily Bonnie had an idea.

She gathered the feathers the chicken had dropped...

She put the sheep
on top of the cow.

She put the pig
on top of the sheep.

Then Bonnie Bumble climbed ...

on top
of the pig

on top
of the sheep

on top
of the cow ...

and tickled
the cloud.

The little cloud giggled
and wriggled and jiggled.

Down came the rain.

The snapdragons beamed.

The tiger lilies purred.

The Johnny jump-ups jumped for joy.

And the black-eyed Susans winked.

All was well again on
Bonnie Bumble's farm.
Except for all the big clouds
that rolled in, and wanted to be
tickled too.

Human Beginnings
in South Africa